by Dache Delaney,
Marques Knight,
Ericka Robinson, &
Dartavius Washington

Drip, Drip.

The Story of the Angry Sherbet

Illustrations by
Carson McNamara

Reach Incorporated | Washington, DC

Shout Mouse Press

Reach Education, Inc. / Shout Mouse Press
Published by
Shout Mouse Press, Inc.

Shout Mouse Press is a nonprofit writing program and publishing house for unheard voices. This book was produced through Shout Mouse workshops and in collaboration with Shout Mouse artists and editors.

Shout Mouse Press empowers writers from marginalized communities to tell their own stories in their own voices and, as published authors, to act as agents of change. In partnership with other nonprofit organizations serving communities in need, we are building a catalog of inclusive, mission-driven books that engage reluctant readers as well as open hearts and minds.

Learn more and see our full catalog at www.shoutmousepress.org.

Copyright © 2016 Reach Education, Inc.
ISBN-13: 978-1945434037 (Shout Mouse Press, Inc.)
ISBN-10: 1945434031

This book is dedicated to the kids
who have problems with anger
and just want to fit in.
You are not alone.

There's a beautiful ice cream shop on the corner of Reach Road. Every day at 6 pm, the kids leave and the owner locks up. But for the rest of the shop, the night has just begun.

"They're gone!" yells Hershey the chocolate bar.

The candies jump out of their boxes and form a line to lift the lid of the ice cream freezer.

One by one, they pull out the treats: vanilla ice cream, chocolate ice cream, banana split. But one little cup is left. Sherbert, the rainbow sherbet cup.

"Can somebody help me get my lid off?" he yells.

Three candy bars come over and lift off his lid.
"Finally! It took you like five seconds!" he says.
"Chill out, man. We had to help everyone else too,"
says Hershey.
"But I'm your best friend! You should have helped
me first."

Drip, drip.

"Sherbert, you're melting. Calm down," says Hershey.

Sherbert and Hershey have known each other since they got shipped in the same box to the ice cream shop. Sherbert was one of the last treats to be loaded onto the truck. The peanuts and whipped cream were already talking to the banana split, the caramel was talking to the chocolate ice cream, and the rainbow sprinkles were talking to the vanilla ice cream. It seemed like everybody had already made a friend. But Sherbert was left alone.

Sherbert felt lonely and angry. He hopped to the corner of the box and slumped down next to Hershey, who was also sitting by himself.

"What's the matter?" Hershey asked.

"Let's just say you should be happy we're in this freezing box or else you would be swimming in a puddle of my ice cream," said Sherbert.

"Do you melt often?" asked Hershey.

"Yeah. I don't know why, I just get angry a lot," said Sherbert.

"I'm not always the happiest chocolate bar either," said Hershey. "I understand."

And from that day on, Sherbert and Hershey have always been together.

Night life at the store is always exciting. Once the owner leaves, the place explodes like Pop Rocks. The ice creams throw a cherry back and forth. Rainbow sprinkles watch and cheer. Jolly Ranchers swim in the milkshake machine.

Sherbert's favorite thing to do is go to the topping dance floor. He watches the cherries, the nuts, and the whipped cream cans dance together. He wishes he could join them.

"Hey Chelsea!" he says to a cherry.

"Hi Sherbert," she says.

"Would you like to be my topping?"

"I'm sorry, but cherries don't go with sherbet..."

And then she bounces away.

Sherbert goes to sit in the corner. He's feeling sad and angry. *Just because I'm sherbet doesn't mean I have to be all alone!* he thinks. As he thinks about how lonely he is, he starts to melt.

Drip, drip.

Hershey looks over and sees Sherbert melting. "Dude, you're dripping!" he says.

"I know! I don't know how to stop it. I'm just so angry," says Sherbert.

"Try this," says Hershey. "Close your eyes and imagine yourself in a frozen place. That's what I do when I get angry."

Sherbert closes his eyes and imagines himself sitting on a frozen beach under an ice-cube sun, watching Hershey ice skate on the frozen waves.

But he can't focus on the beach. He can't get the image of Chelsea rejecting him out of his head.

While Sherbert is talking to Hershey, there is a meeting going on in the fridge.

"Why is Sherbert always so grumpy? It makes everyone sad," says the banana split.

"And what if he gets angry and melts and there's a big puddle on the floor? If the owner comes in and sees it, then we're all creamed!" yells Vanilla.

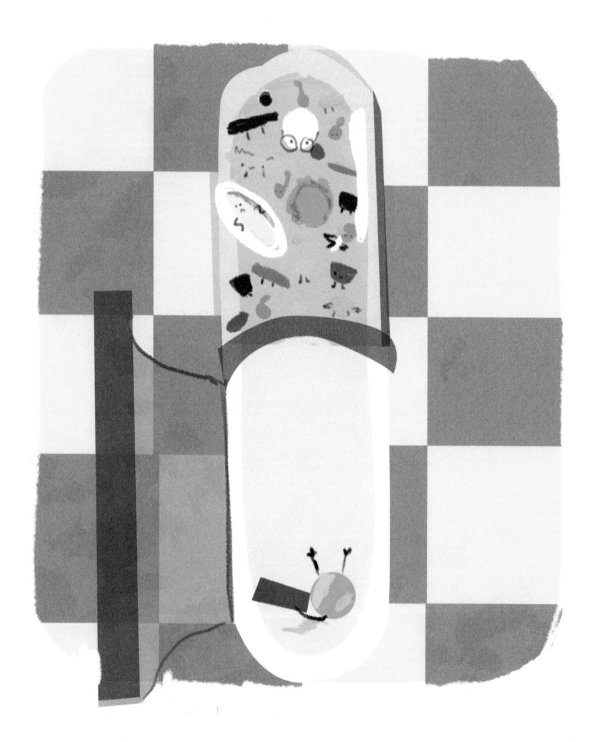

"What's happening over there? Let's go check it out," asks Sherbert.

"Noooo, let's just stay here," says Hershey.

As Sherbert enters the fridge, everyone starts leaving.

"What's going on? Where are you going?" he asks.

Nobody answers.

Sherbert starts to get mad.

"It was probably nothing," says Hershey. "Let's just go back to the corner."

Sherbert looks around. "Why does everyone look like they're giving me the cold shoulder?"

Drip, drip.

Sherbert is melting.

"Look at you! You're getting all over the floor. Come on, let's go back to the freezer," says Hershey.

"No! Leave me alone!"

"Don't you like it here? If they catch us, then we won't be able to go out at night anymore. And if you melt, the owner will just throw you away! You need to learn how to control your anger."

"Fine, what do you suggest?!" says Sherbert.

"Taking deep breaths is always the first step to feeling better. Breathe in through your nose and out through your mouth. Come on, let's try it together."

Sherbert takes a deep breath. After five breaths, he feels a little better, but he is still dripping. Nothing seems to work.

"OK, let's get you back to the freezer," says Hershey. He picks Sherbert up and takes him to cool down.

As dawn starts to break, everyone heads back to their sections. The owner comes in and sees little droplets of ice cream on the floor. "Those darn kids," he mutters and mops it up. The candies all breathe a sigh of relief.

"That was close," Hershey says to Sherbert.

"TOO close!" Vanilla says angrily. "Keep it together, Sherbert!"

The other icecreams agree and then get ready for their day-time nap.

They all go to sleep and wait for nightfall.

All except Sherbert.

Sherbert is too angry to sleep.

That night, everyone gets in their groups. Sherbert and Hershey walk past the Laffy Taffys, who are reading each other's jokes.

"Everybody hates me. And none of your stupid ideas work," says Sherbert. "Nothing I do ever helps me stop melting."

Hershey replies, "I'm just trying to be your friend and help you out. But maybe you're not trying hard enough."

Sherbert can feel the drips coming. "I don't need you!" he says.

"Well, you need to find something to control your anger," says Hershey.

"You don't know what you're talking about! You're just a stupid chocolate bar!" yells Sherbert. "You don't melt like I do!"

"Actually, I do melt!" yells Hershey. "Why do you think I have so much advice for you? But I guess you're too hung up in your drama to realize that. You know what? Fine. Let's see how you manage on your own."

And then he leaves.

Sherbert sits alone. They're all just a bunch of Nerds, he thinks. They talk about me behind my back, like I don't know they don't want to be my friend. And they think they're going to get the best of me?!

Drip, drip.

As Sherbert gets angrier and angrier, he starts melting all over the floor. He looks down into the puddle of himself and sees his face. It's an "I've-lost-my-best-friend" face.

He tries to hop, but there is a big splash. The puddle is soaking through the bottom of his cup. He starts to panic. *I really need to get back to the freezer, or I'll disappear completely,* he thinks. But he can't calm down enough to stop melting.

Sherbert looks at the freezer, but it seems so far away. How long will it take him to get back?

He begins to count the tiles on the floor.

One, two, three, four.

He starts to hop, and with each hop he counts.

Five, six, seven, eight.

On the tenth hop he looks back and realizes that with each hop, the puddles behind him are getting smaller. It seem like the counting has taken his mind off what he's angry about. He finally found something that calms him down!

Eleven, twelve, thirteen hops.

Finally, he is back at the freezer. He yells up to get Hershey's attention. "Hershey!"

But Hershey doesn't answer.

"Hershey, I'm sorry! I really need your help! I was wrong earlier. You're more than a chocolate bar. You're my best friend."

He waits, but Hershey still doesn't answer.

"I know I get angry a lot, so I took your advice. I found a way to control myself. Some of your techniques didn't work for me, but I found something that did!"

Finally, Hershey comes out. "Ok, Sherbert. I accept your apology. I'm glad you owned up to being angry. And that's great that you found something that works for you! I'll always be here for you. That's what best friends are for."

He whistles loudly, and all of the candies peek out. "Chocolates, line up! Let's get to work!"

The chocolates line up with tiny mops. "Clean up time, clean up time, everybody hop in line," they sing. By the end of the song, the sherbet on the floor is gone.

"Thank you for cleaning up," Sherbert says. "I get really upset sometimes because I feel left out, but I'm finding ways to deal with it and be more chill."

"I understand," says Chelsea the cherry. "Everyone gets upset sometimes, even me."

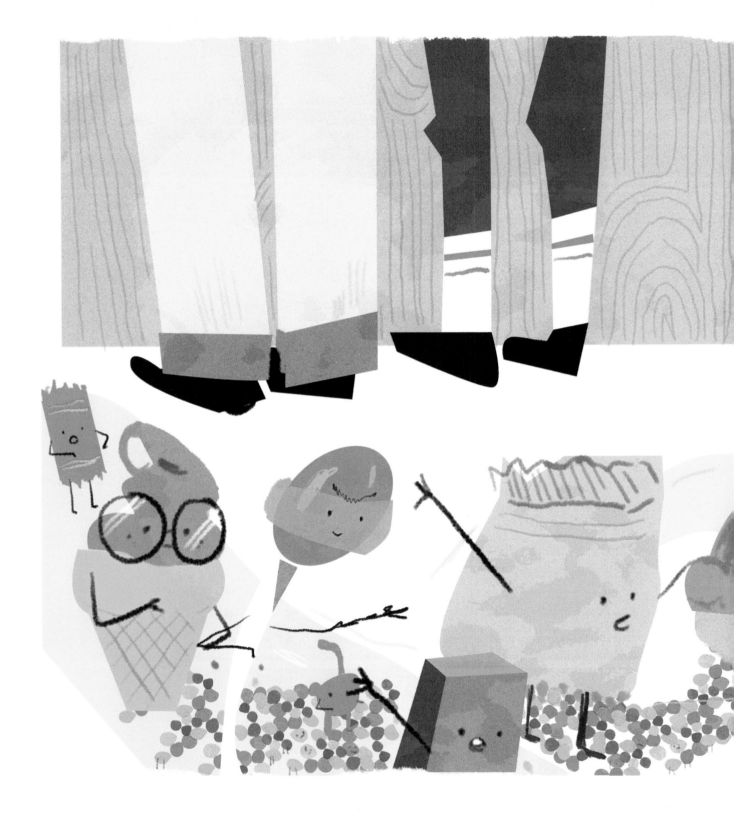

Jingle jingle. "Keys! Keys! Keys! Keys!" peep a hundred Nerds, jumping up and down.

The chocolates scramble to open the lid of the freezer and Sherbert hops in. Everyone goes back to their shelves.

The door swings open and the owner walks in, followed by two little kids.

"May I have some sherbet?" says one of the kids.

"I'd like a chocolate bar, please," says the other.

Fun Fact
for curious readers

Sherbert is most commonly spelled "sherbet," which is pronounced "sherbit." It is an icy treat made of milk, sugar, and fruit. It comes from the Arabic word "sharbah," which means "a drink." Many dictionaries recognize the spellings "sherbert" as well as "sherbet" because it is so commonly mispronounced in the English language. We chose to name Sherbert "Sherbert" and describe him as "sherbet" to acknowledge both spellings of the word.

About the Authors

DACHE DELANEY
is from Washington, DC and is a junior at McKinley Tech High School. She loves sherbet, which was an inspiration to come up with the main character, Sherbert. Writing this book was a way for her to bring all of her favorite treats to life while also making a connection to her real life troubles with anger.

MARQUES KNIGHT
is an 18-year-old senior from Washington, DC who was originally from Detroit. He goes to Ballou Senior High School. He will eat sherbet more than ice cream any day. He likes to read, draw, play games, and play chess. Marques is also a co-author of *A to Z: The Real DC*. He wrote that book to help kids learn about their city and hopefully to get them to go out and explore. He has had a lot of fun writing books and hopes to continue.

ERICKA ROBINSON

is from Washington, DC and currently lives in the Southeast area. She is a senior at Ballou Senior High School. She loves to write, which was the main reason she decided to help write this story. This is her first children's book, and she hopes to one day write a novel and be a lawyer. Creating the plot of this story was fun because she got to explore the world of not people or animals, but sweet treats!

DARTAVIUS WASHINGTON

is a 15-year-old sophomore at Dunbar High School in Washington, DC. This is his first book with Reach. His dream is to become an NBA legend or an actor. He liked working on this story with his peers and felt very bright during this process. He would like kids to understand that every situation isn't worth getting mad at or crying over.

RACHEL PAGE served as Story Scribe for this book.
KATHY CRUTCHER served as Story Coach and Series Editor.

About the Illustrator

CARSON MCNAMARA

is an illustrator based in her hometown of Richmond, VA. She's a Communication Arts student at Virginia Commonwealth University, a bookseller, and an avid reader who thinks all books would be better with pictures. She loves using illustration to clarify and enhance someone's story, and working on projects with groups like Shout Mouse where illustration can represent all people and be a force for good. You can see more of her work at carsonmcnamara.com.

Writers and artists at work

Acknowledgments

For the fourth summer in a row, teens from Reach Incorporated were issued a challenge: compose original children's books that will both educate and entertain young readers. Specifically, these teens were asked to create inclusive stories that reflect the realities of their communities, so that every child has the opportunity to relate to characters on the page. And for the fourth summer in a row, these teens have demonstrated that they know their audience, they believe in their mission, and they take pride in the impact they can make on young lives.

Fourteen writers spent the month of July brainstorming ideas, generating potential plots, writing, revising, and providing critiques. Authoring quality books is challenging work, and these authors have our immense gratitude and respect: Rochelle, Destiney, Naseem, Darrin, Aderemi, Taijah, Abreona, Temil, Marques, Ericka, Dartavius, Dache, Kairon, and R.E.L.

These books represent a collaboration between Reach Incorporated and Shout Mouse Press, and we are grateful for the leadership provided by members of both teams. From Reach, D'Juan Thomas contributed meaningfully to discussions and morale, and the Reach summer program leadership kept us organized and well-equipped. From the Shout Mouse Press team, we thank Story Coach Hayes Davis and Story Scribes Sarai Johnson, Barrett Smith, Andi Mirviss, Eva Shapiro, and Rachel Page for bringing both fun and insight to the project. We can't thank enough illustrators Evey Cahall, Carson McNamara, Jamilla Okubo, and Zoe Gatti for bringing these stories to life with their beautiful artwork. We are grateful for the time and talents of these writers and artists!

Finally, we thank those of you who have purchased books and cheered on our authors. It is your support that makes it possible for these teen authors to engage and inspire young readers. We hope you smile as much while you read as these teens did while they wrote.

Mark Hecker,
Reach Incorporated

Kathy Crutcher,
Shout Mouse Press

About Reach Incorporated

Reach Incorporated develops grade-level readers and capable leaders by preparing teens to serve as tutors and role models for younger students, resulting in improved literacy outcomes for both.

Founded in 2009, Reach recruits high school students to be elementary school reading tutors. Elementary school students average 1.5 grade levels of reading growth per year of participation. This growth – equal to that created by highly effective teachers – is created by high school students who average more than two grade levels of growth per year of program participation.

As skilled reading tutors, our teens noticed that the books they read with their students did not reflect their reality. As always, we felt the best way we could address this issue was to let our teen tutors author new books. Through our collaboration with Shout Mouse Press, these teens create fanciful stories with diverse characters that invite young readers to explore the world through words. By purchasing our books, you support student-led, community-driven efforts to improve educational outcomes in the District of Columbia.

Learn more at www.reachincorporated.org

CPSIA information can be obtained
at www.ICGtesting.com
Printed in the USA
LVOW05s0137230218
567650LV00015B/59/P